Touch the Moon

Touch the Moon

Marion Dane Bauer

drawings by Alix Berenzy

CLARION BOOKS
TICKNOR & FIELDS: A HOUGHTON MIFFLIN COMPANY
NEW YORK

Clarion Books
a Houghton Mifflin Company imprint
215 Park Avenue South, New York, NY 10003
Text copyright © 1987 by Marion Dane Bauer
Illustrations copyright © 1987 by Alix Berenzy
Printed in the U.S.A.

Library of Congress Cataloging-in-Publication Data
Bauer, Marion Dane.
  Touch the moon.
  Summary: When the china horse Jennifer receives for
her birthday is magically transformed into a real
horse, they share an evening of fantastic adventures.
  [1. Horses—Fiction. 2. Magic—Fiction] I. Title.
PZ7.B3262To 1987   [Fic]   87-663
ISBN 0-89919-526-1

VB   10   9   8   7   6

For Jo

Touch the Moon

chapter one

Jennifer picked up the small package, the last of her birthday gifts, the one from her father. She flashed a smile in his direction, and her happiness bounced back across the table to her from his broad, friendly face. She had waited forever for this moment, to be eleven years old and to get a horse for her birthday.

Of course she knew her horse wouldn't be in this tiny box. She almost giggled at the idea. But she had asked—in fact she had asked and asked and asked—and her father had finally agreed that when she was eleven she would be old enough for a real horse.

Jennifer smoothed the delicately flowered gift wrap, her hand trembling just slightly. Maybe the small box would hold a photo of a golden palomino with cream-colored mane and tail. It would be a picture of the horse she had already named Pretty Girl, the one who was waiting for her, hidden away somewhere. Maybe it held a message telling her where to look . . . in the garage, perhaps, or within the triangle of enormous spruce trees in the backyard. Or her horse might be stabled at a farm outside of town, and this was the key to the stall. There must be a hundred funny, wonderful ways her father could let her know that Pretty Girl was hers at last.

Jennifer's mother didn't understand about horses, about how important they were, but her father did. He always had.

Jennifer's mother was beginning to stack the dishes, reaching from where she sat. She acted almost as if the birthday were already over, as though the biggest moment weren't still to come. Her grandmother sipped coffee, her eyes crinkled above her steaming cup. Brad, Jennifer's twelve-year-old brother, poked his finger into the remains of the chocolate cake and came away with a glob of frosting. He crossed his eyes at Jennifer, obviously bored and wanting to go watch television. But then he probably hadn't guessed what was in this last box. He had never believed Daddy was going to get her a horse anyway.

With great care, without hurrying even a little, Jennifer began lifting the tape at one end of the small package. She would keep this violet-sprigged paper, show it to her best friend, Liz, the next day. She would tell her, *This is the gift wrap that came on my horse!*

Wouldn't that make Liz laugh?

Jennifer folded the paper back, revealing a nubbly, cream-colored box, exactly the color Pretty Girl's mane was going to be. Slowly, she lifted the lid. The container was filled with shredded paper almost like straw, and Jennifer pushed her empty cake plate aside and set the small box on the table in front of her. She used two fingers to separate the paper straw.

Something cool and smooth was hidden in the packing, and Jennifer drew it out carefully, holding her breath. It was a china horse, about three inches tall . . . her horse exactly. She couldn't have imagined a miniature more exactly like the horse she had dreamed. It was a palomino with a golden coat and a creamy mane and a tail like a riffling flag. The tiny horse ran on thin, thin legs, its nostrils flaring, its head tossed with pride. *Ride me if you dare,* it seemed to say.

"Oh, Daddy!" She held the china figurine carefully on the flat of her hand. "It's the most beautiful horse I've ever seen." There was a note lying at the bottom of the box, the note Jennifer had been expecting, but she didn't want to look at that yet. Now that Pretty Girl was almost hers, she wanted to stretch out the final delicious moments of waiting.

She held her hand up higher so Brad could see the statuette, and he looked at it without interest. *Big deal,* she could almost hear him thinking, *a toy horse.* She smiled to think how his face would change when she read out the note.

3

"You've seen that horse before, you know," her father was saying. "It was on the windowsill halfway up the stairs at Grandma's house." And then he added softly, "When I was a boy I used to ride the bannister, pretending it was that horse grown large."

Jennifer studied the figurine. Was it possible that she had seen it before, a horse so like the one she always pretended to ride? There were no stairs in her house, so she and Liz each straddled a branch in one of the spruce trees out back. Liz's horse was glisteningly black with a white blaze on his face, but Pretty Girl looked exactly like the one Jennifer held in her hand.

"That little horse has been packed away for a long time," her grandmother added. "When I moved to the apartment and didn't have room for so many of my things, I kept it in the box, tucked away in a drawer." She smiled in Jennifer's father's direction and added, softly, "Your daddy used to love it so."

Jennifer stroked the glassy back of the figurine. She glanced again at the folded note in the bottom of the box.

"My brother made fun of me for being such a dreamer," her father said. "He couldn't understand why I wanted to ride a bannister horse." He ducked his head, chuckled softly, and smoothed his napkin with great care.

Jennifer gave Brad a knowing look. He had teased her, too . . . lots of times, but he wouldn't make fun anymore, not when he saw her real birthday present.

She set the tiny horse on the table in front of her and picked up the note, unfolding it with deliberate care.

It read:

Dear Jennifer,
    Beginning Saturday morning, you are enrolled for weekly horseback riding lessons at Sunny Acres Farm.
    Happy birthday!
                            Love,
                            Daddy

Jennifer read the note three times, holding her back carefully erect, her hands still. Was this all? No horse of her own, only riding lessons?

She didn't want riding lessons. She didn't *need* riding lessons. She had spent half her life practicing, and all she needed was a horse! Surely her father knew that. She looked at him to see if there was some mistake.

Happiness was glowing behind the blue sky of his eyes, as if riding lessons were the most wonderful gift of all. As if riding lessons were what she had asked for.

She looked around the table. Everyone was watching her. Everyone was waiting for her to be grateful and pleased.

She folded the square of paper carefully, put it back into the box.

"Jennifer's going to start riding lessons," her father explained to anyone at the table who didn't already know, filling in her silence for her.

Jennifer looked one more time at Brad, expecting him to say something obnoxious. *Big deal!* maybe. *I told you so,* at least.

"Daddy never got a real horse," Brad had said over and over again, "so why should you get one?" And he had said other things, too, about how much money horses cost . . . to buy, to feed. About how much work they were to clean up after . . . all that expensive feed coming out the other end. About how it was probably illegal to have a horse in town anyway.

But Brad grinned and gave her a thumbs up, as if riding lessons might be the best birthday present in the world.

Jennifer struggled to her feet. Her face felt numb. "Thank you, Daddy," she said in a voice like a squeezed balloon. "Your horse is beautiful. But I guess I'll have to think about the lessons."

Her father looked surprised, even hurt, but before he could say anything more she picked up the tiny horse and walked, robotlike, out of the dining room. She passed through the kitchen, littered with the preparations for her big birthday dinner—who wanted a birthday, anyway?—and pushed out the door.

chapter two

Jennifer sat perched high in one of the spruce trees, higher, in fact, than she had ever been before. She looked down into the large enclosure formed by the three trees. They had been planted only about six feet apart, so as they grew, the inside limbs had shriveled for lack of sun, leaving the space between them a shadowy cavern. That cavern and the thick trees themselves were a perfect hiding spot as well as a place for pretending. Not that she was ever going to come out here to pretend to ride again. All that was ruined now.

She sat with her back snug against the trunk, unmindful of the sticky sap which would probably stain her new pink slacks and shirt, her birthday present from her mother. What did she care if they were ruined? It wasn't fair for parents to give clothes for birthdays anyway. They had to buy their kids clothes . . . unless they wanted them running around naked.

Her grandmother's gift, a lavender scarf knitted out of soft angora, was wrapped loosely around her neck. The scarf was the nicest present she could remember getting from her grandmother, but it wasn't much use in the middle of summer. Grandma never paid any attention to seasons. Usually she knitted Jennifer a pair of mittens for her July birthday, made out of scraps and bits of leftover yarn. Jennifer brushed the softness of the angora scarf against her cheek. It was definitely better than multicolored mittens.

Then she touched the bicycle lamp clipped to her belt, her present from Brad. She liked that, too, even though it wasn't of much use. Her parents wouldn't let her go out with her bike after dark. She unclipped the light and looked at it carefully. The reflector around the bulb was slightly rusty. Brad had probably rescued her birthday present from somebody's trash.

She didn't mind that. In some families parents supplied money for kids to buy one another gifts, but not in theirs. Last year Brad had given her a bowl of tadpoles gathered from the marshy backwaters of the nearby river. The tadpoles all died before they turned into frogs, which was probably just as well. While she was waiting for them to grow legs, she had dreams about waking up to tiny frogs hopping all over her face.

She flipped the switch, and the lamp came on. (Brad must

have *bought* new batteries or taken the batteries out of one of his toys.) The beam of light barely penetrated the green shadow of the surrounding trees, though. It would be brighter when the sun went all the way down. She had never understood how light swallowed up light. It seemed as though darkness would do that.

Jennifer clicked off the bicycle lamp, clipped it onto her belt again, and turned with a sigh to her father's gift, the china horse. She had balanced it on the branch a short distance from where she sat, and it stood there, or rather seemed to be running there, frozen in midstride. The tail flowed straight out behind and the mane rippled in the wind of its running. The head was held high and turned slightly to one side, as if the horse were ready to come alive, to change direction and leap off the branch.

Jennifer reached toward the figurine, forming her middle finger and thumb into a circle. With a single flick she could knock her father's gift off the branch, watch it fall to the hard ground below. The silly thing would probably break into a million pieces if she did, despite the cushion of needles on the ground. Having his precious toy smashed would be no more than her father deserved anyway. What right did he have to give her riding lessons when he had promised a horse!

Her father *had* promised, hadn't he? Jennifer let her hand drop to her lap. She tried to remember his exact words. "On your eleventh birthday you'll be big enough to ride a real horse." That was what he had said. She sat erect as if pulled up straight by her hair. He had kept his promise . . . or at least he thought he had. To him the important word was *ride*. And that was what he had given her, riding lessons. Shouldn't someone, though, who had spent years dreaming of his very own horse have known that the important word was *horse*?

Jennifer swiped at her stinging eyes. It wasn't fair. He had spoiled everything. She wouldn't even be able to enjoy pretending anymore . . . she had been so sure that by this evening Pretty Girl would be hers. She had even told Liz that they would be able to ride for real tomorrow, that they would ride out of the city, through fields, over fences, and it wouldn't be pretend.

She reached again and, with her index finger, stroked the back of the tiny horse. The figure was so perfectly formed that she could almost feel the muscles flex beneath the hard surface.

She ran her finger down the horse's neck. Here she could definitely feel the tendons standing out, the effort of the running, the proud lift of the head.

She sighed, leaned back against the tree trunk. "All I wanted in the whole world," she said out loud to the fragrant green gloom, "was a real horse."

She had been on a horse, a live horse, only once in her life. It had been a carnival pony last summer, not much better than a merry-go-round horse really. The little pony

had been attached to a long pole like a wheel spoke, so it had to walk in an endless, dusty circle. Liz had laughed because the poor thing had been so small that Jennifer's feet nearly dragged on the ground. (Liz had refused to ride, had said the ponies were meant for little kids.) Still, the pony Jennifer had ridden had the good, nose-twitching smell of a real horse . . . and he had eaten a piece of apple out of her hand after the ride exactly as any big horse might have done.

Jennifer could still almost feel the softness of the pony's nose, the tickling spikes of whiskers, the great, warm puffs of breath that flooded her palm. Pretty Girl would have smelled like that, and she would have had the same velvet nose, too, the soft, leathery lips, and breath like freshly mown grass.

"I wish . . ." Jennifer whispered, but then she stopped. How did the people in the fairy stories do it? She had been wishing for a horse, talking about a horse, pretending she had a horse forever, and nothing was changed. Nothing.

In the stories, someone powerful always made the wish come true. Or the person found a magic ring . . . or a magic china horse. Jennifer picked up the statuette, then set it down again.

The wishes in stories never did anybody any good anyway. The people who were granted their wish—or three—wasted them nearly every time. And they were never smart enough to ask the only sensible thing with their first try, that *all* their wishes would come true so they could keep on wishing until things turned out right.

Jennifer squeezed her eyes shut. If she concentrated very hard, maybe . . .

But there was nothing to see behind her closed lids except blackness, then gradually, the way it always did, the blackness began to grow lighter around the edges. Colors flowed across her vision . . . red, then green, then a creamy white, the color of Pretty Girl's mane.

Jennifer rubbed her eye sockets with her fists, opened her eyes. She was never going to dream anything again . . . ever. Her father could dream if he wanted to. He was an architect, and he was always saying that dreams were important. He dreamed up buildings for people to live in, to work in. But he hadn't done a thing to make her dream of a horse come true.

She stared at the running figure balanced on the branch, holding its head at an arrogant angle, flaunting its tail.

"I don't believe in dreams," Jennifer said to the horse. "I don't believe in anything." She felt very grown-up as she said it. Rather empty inside, but very grown-up.

And knowing that her father's china horse would only remind her continually of that emptiness, she reached out with one finger and tipped it off the branch.

She watched the fragile figure fall, saw it spin and plummet in the dusky light. About halfway down it bounced off a stunted inner branch and disappeared in the shadows.

Jennifer leaned forward, listening for the sharp, satisfying clunk which would signal the breaking. She heard only a cricket chirping beyond the trees and a car humming past on the street in front of the house. A dog barked somewhere far away. Then everything was silent. There was not even the faint whisper of a breeze passing through the evergreen branches.

The horse must be shattered. The ground was so far away. Jennifer peered into the shadows, trying to feel relieved. There was nothing to see except a swirling golden mist, apparently some trick of the setting sun filtering through the trees.

She drew in a deep breath, trying to feel glad that the silly thing was gone. Then she stopped, breathed again, a long, wavering breath this time. Something was wrong. China horses had no smell. Even a broken china horse couldn't possibly have a smell. But here she was . . . invaded, surrounded, overwhelmed by the odor of horse!

And by strange sounds as well. The splintering crunch of branches breaking, snorting breath, stamping feet.

She blinked, leaned over farther. Below her, contained by the enclosing branches of the three enormous trees, the mist seemed to be solidifying, taking on shape. And the shape was most definitely that of a horse!

Jennifer clung to the tree, staring. It was the most beautiful horse she had ever seen. Its coat gleamed like burnished gold, and its mane and tail were the color of thick cream. Muscles rippled beneath the golden coat, and the horse half reared, tossing its head. It lashed out with sharp hooves and shattered the brittle, dead limbs that extended into the enclosure. Once it kicked the trunk of the tree Jennifer was in, making the branch she was sitting on tremble.

But even more astonishing than the appearance of the horse, its beauty and violent energy, was the thing she had noticed first. Its smell. It was rich and full . . . and real. It filled Jennifer's nose, her lungs, her entire body, the way her father's promise had once filled her dreams. No dream horse could smell like that.

Pretty Girl! Here, at last, was Pretty Girl in the flesh!

chapter three

Jennifer scrambled down a few branches to get closer to the beautiful horse. Pretty Girl tossed her finely sculpted head and half reared, trying to free herself from the branches which thrust, sharp and needleless, from the inner trunks of the spruce trees.

Jennifer stopped just above the horse's head and gaped, too stunned to know what she should do. Pretty Girl went on twisting and thrashing about, colliding with branches and occasionally with the trunk of one of the trees. "Stop!" Jennifer called out, as if it were any use to talk to a horse. "Be careful! You'll hurt yourself!"

Where had Pretty Girl come from? But of course, she knew the answer to that. From her father! Where else? The note about the riding lessons was only a kind of teasing, a setting up for the surprise. He had wanted her to think that the china horse was the only horse she would get, at least for the length of time it took to bring Pretty Girl here.

"Oh, Daddy, thank you!" Jennifer called, though she didn't see where her father was standing. Right outside the trees, no doubt. Probably the whole family was standing there, waiting to see how surprised she would be.

But her father didn't answer, and Pretty Girl continued to toss her head, whickering and half lifting her front legs from the ground, fighting against the enclosing branches. Jennifer looked down at the broad golden back. She hadn't expected her horse to be so big!

"Daddy?" she called again, hating the bit of a quaver she could hear in her own voice. She wished she had a rope. She could loop it around Pretty Girl's neck and then . . . and then she didn't know what she would do next. She hadn't wanted a little Shetland pony like the one in the carnival, but this enormous creature was almost too much. If she got down onto the ground next to those hooves, she would be kicked or stepped on for sure.

"Dad!" she yelled at the top of her lungs.

"I am not your father" came the response, musical and high, but penetratingly loud.

Jennifer gasped for breath and grabbed, again, for the trunk of the tree. She looked around for the source of the voice, but saw nothing, no one . . . only the gigantic, rearing, stamping horse.

"Why did you bring me in here?" the voice asked querulously. "There's not enough room in here for a horse of my size." And as if to prove the point, Pretty Girl kicked out with powerful hind legs and broke three low branches.

Jennifer had to wrap both arms around the trunk to keep from toppling out of the tree. Excitement and fear raced through her bones.

"Daddy!" she squeaked, one last time, but even as she spoke, she knew with absolute certainty that her father was nowhere around. This horse, this *talking* horse, must have arrived entirely on its own. Could its appearance have something to do with the china figure she had tipped off the branch? That didn't seem possible, but who was to say what was possible about a *talking* horse?

Jennifer loosened her grip enough to peer down again at the creature below her. Having wanted a horse for so long, she couldn't afford to be picky about how it arrived . . . or whether or not it talked. Still, she had the odd feeling of being caught in a dream she hadn't chosen.

"If you'll hold still," she said, her voice really quavering this time, "I'll help you."

Pretty Girl stopped rearing, stopped tossing her head about. One great hoof pawed the ground smartly but then that quieted, too. "Well, you'd better," the great horse said, not at all graciously.

Jennifer ignored the tone and climbed the rest of the way down. When she dropped to the ground and turned to look at the animal towering above her there in the confines of her own little hideout, she had to close her eyes for a moment. Pretty Girl was huge! But then, since there was nothing else to be done, she opened them again and moved tentatively toward the horse's head. *Wait till Liz sees this!* she thought, keeping close watch on the slender but powerful legs, on the large hooves. "It's all right," she said as she sidled along. "Just hold very still."

Pretty Girl merely snorted in response, but the snort seemed to say she didn't think anything was the least bit all right.

"Maybe if I hold the branches for you," Jennifer said when she stood beside the massive head, "you can follow me out."

Pretty Girl, if that's who this horse was, eyed the branches Jennifer was separating. "I'm much bigger than that," she said.

"All you have to do is to push past them. It's nothing but a spruce tree." Jennifer spoke in a soothing voice suitable for addressing a very small child, not an enormous beast several times her own size. At the same time she tried to hold the branches farther apart.

"They'll snap back on me. They'll close me in." Pretty Girl stamped her feet again, and Jennifer retreated rapidly.

"Be still," she said sharply. "If you'll be still, I'll get you out."

She almost added, *you big baby,* but she looked at the massive chest, the sharp hooves and fierce, white teeth and

she didn't. "Maybe I could find a rope in the garage," she offered.

"What good would that do?" Pretty Girl snarled.

"Well, I could put it around your neck and pull—"

Pretty Girl shook herself violently, and when her flying mane had settled again, Jennifer added quickly, "I don't suppose that would help."

"I don't suppose it would," the horse agreed dryly, and Jennifer looked around for some other solution. There was, of course, nothing to be seen but the enclosing branches of the trees, and they were, themselves, the problem.

She thought of going in to get her father, but she didn't want to leave. What if Pretty Girl disappeared as magically as she had come? And what if her father asked her what she had done to his china figurine to turn it into this incredible horse? Could she tell him she had knocked it off the branch, that she had wanted to break it?

Then she had another idea.

"Put your head down," she ordered. She had seen this done on TV once, when a horse had to be led out of a burning barn, though of course on TV they hadn't been able to tell the horse what to do.

"Why should I?" Pretty Girl demanded.

Jennifer almost smiled. At least such bad manners proved, if she needed proof, that Pretty Girl was real. No one would imagine any animal so contrary. "Because," she replied, trying to sound as much like an exasperated parent as possible, "if you don't do what I say, I'll go off and leave you caught in this place forever."

She could tell Pretty Girl was considering that possibility. "And if I do what you say?" It seemed to be a genuine question.

"Then I'll get you out, and we can go for a run. Anyplace you like."

Pretty Girl tossed her head, but then, to Jennifer's surprise, she lowered it. Her satin brown eyes peered at Jennifer through heavy lashes, and she asked in a voice that was almost meek, "What are you going to do to me?"

"Just this." And Jennifer pulled off her new angora scarf and wrapped it tightly around Pretty Girl's head, covering the watching eyes. She tied a knot below the huge jaws.

"It's dark," Pretty Girl complained in a small, almost trembly voice.

"No, it's not dark. It's not dark at all. It's just like you have your eyes closed, and while your eyes are closed, I'll get you safely out of here."

"Well, you'd better," Pretty Girl replied, thrusting out her lips in an immense pout.

For a moment Jennifer stood there, facing the blindfolded horse, thinking, *Why am I doing this? I don't owe this rude beast a thing!*

But then she thought of the wonderful gallop they would have the moment they were out and away from the trees. She reached up, took hold of the creamy forelock and began to push her way through the intertwined branches.

"Follow me," she said gruffly, and the gigantic animal followed. In fact, the horse pushed through the branches exactly as she could have done with her eyes open if she hadn't been so inexplicably afraid.

Jennifer looked back at Pretty Girl, and her chest swelled with pride. Rude or not, scared or not, this was *her* horse at last.

chapter four

"Okay. You're all right now," Jennifer said when Pretty Girl had emerged unharmed onto the open lawn.

She gazed at the huge animal. What would her parents say when they saw her? Would they tell Jennifer she couldn't keep any horse no matter how it had arrived? She wasn't going to take any chances. She would make sure this birthday present wasn't seen. Fortunately, they had come out into the yard on the side away from the house, between the trees and a tall wooden fence which separated their backyard from the neighbor's.

Jennifer reached up and untied her new scarf from around Pretty Girl's eyes, and the horse shook her head and stamped one front hoof smartly. Then instead of thanking Jennifer for her help, the ungrateful animal said, "Don't you ever do that again!"

Jennifer was astonished. "Do what? Rescue you when you're scared?"

Pretty Girl snorted. "Scared? Who says I was scared? I'm a stallion, and stallions aren't afraid of anything." And the stallion, if that was what he was, tossed his head until his mane flew about wildly.

Jennifer didn't see why stallions couldn't be as afraid as anyone else. This horse's boasting reminded her of Brad and his friends when they were trying to prove how tough they were. Still, she decided the subject was best dropped. "How come you can talk?" she asked, beginning to walk around Pretty Girl so she could view her from every side. No, him. Apparently she would have to reconsider the name.

"Why shouldn't I be able to talk? You talk!"

"But I'm a girl . . . a human being. You're a horse."

"A stallion," he corrected.

"A stallion," she conceded from the perspective of his back side. "But stallions don't talk either."

"Who says so? How many stallions have you met?"

Jennifer thought about that and decided that she hadn't met any. Still she was certain that being a stallion—a kind of father horse—didn't mean an animal would be able to talk. She decided to try a different topic.

"What's your name?" she asked, returning to the horse's head. Obviously the name Pretty Girl would not do, and somehow Pretty Boy just didn't have the same ring.

"Name? Am I supposed to have a name?"

Jennifer smiled. At last she had the upper hand. "You mean you don't know your own name?" she asked, putting just the right inflection in her voice to match his earlier snideness.

The nameless horse turned in place, apparently considering. He ended up facing the trees. "How about Spruce Tree," he suggested.

"For a name?" She suppressed most of a giggle.

He was clearly offended by the part of the giggle that had leaked out. He looked over his shoulder and curled his upper lip in a way which would have been quite menacing if they hadn't been in the middle of such a peculiar discussion.

Jennifer said quickly, "If you're going to be my horse . . . my stallion," she corrected herself, "then I should get to name you."

"Yours? What makes you think you can own me?" Spruce Tree, if that was who he was going to be, began to prance sideways. He moved toward the middle of the yard, looking at her with obvious distaste.

"Don't go over there!" Jennifer called after him. She had a sudden vision of her mother standing at the kitchen sink and looking out into the backyard.

He stopped prancing. "Why not?" He didn't move an inch back toward her and the sheltering trees.

"Because *they* might see you," she whispered urgently. It occurred to her for the first time that the windows would all be open and that there was as much risk they might be heard as seen.

"Nobody can see *me*," the horse said, but still he threw an uneasy look around the yard and stepped quickly and, Jennifer was glad to note, quietly, back to her side. "Who are *they*?" He kept his voice low.

"My parents," Jennifer answered, ignoring his pretense that he couldn't be seen. He was the most *seeable* horse she could imagine. "If they see you, they might send you back."

"Back where?" He dropped his head to peer intently into her face.

Jennifer shrugged. She didn't know back where. "Where you came from, I suppose."

The horse said nothing.

"Where *did* you come from?" she asked.

There was another long pause, then he answered, sounding a bit bewildered, "I don't think I know."

The stallion's uncertainty pleased Jennifer. Up till now he had been such a know-it-all horse! His having no idea where he came from pleased her, too, because no one could send him back without that information. "Well, how long have you been here?" she asked, figuring he would know more about that.

"Oh, a long time." His head rose to its usual prideful height. "At least ten minutes, I'd say. Maybe fifteen."

Jennifer laughed out loud. This gigantic horse was a baby!

The stallion twitched his ears irritably. "There was something before this. I'm just not sure what it was."

"I'm sure there was," Jennifer said reassuringly, and then,

wanting to get the preliminaries taken care of so they could go for a ride, she added, "It's fine to pick your own name, but can't you think of something better than Spruce Tree?"

The horse made another revolution in the grass. "What's that?" he asked, nodding toward the garage.

"It's a garage," Jennifer replied, and then before he could try it out, she added quickly, "and Garage isn't a good name either." *Neither is Driveway,* she almost added, *or Fence,* but decided she had best leave well enough alone lest he found one of those irresistible. She could just imagine riding a horse named Driveway.

The nameless horse took a mouthful of grass and began to munch loudly. "It seems to me I had a name once," he said somewhat indistinctly over the sound of chewing, "something like— Criminey!"

"Criminey! What an odd name. My father's the only person in the whole world who says that." It was a word her father used when he was startled . . . or worried . . . or angry. He said it on all kinds of occasions, actually.

"No . . . no. That isn't what I meant. I was just remembering. My name. It had to do with looking for something . . . up there." He cast his eyes toward the sky.

"Star," Jennifer said impatiently. "Your name must be Starfinder." If they didn't get away from here pretty quickly, her mother would come out and call her in.

"No." He shook his head firmly. "That's not it."

Jennifer sighed, then tipped her head back and gazed into

the sky herself, trying to think of something else. But there was nothing to see. The sunset was fading and even the blue was draining from the sky, so there was only a kind of pale blank overhead.

"Spoon, loon, dune," the horse muttered. "Croon."

And Jennifer answered immediately, "Moon.... Of course!" But then she offered, less certainly, "Moonlooker?"

"No!" He shook his head. "But you're right about the moon part. That's what it was. Moon . . . something."

Jennifer was surprised he would admit she had gotten anything right, but she didn't have another idea in her head. She closed her eyes and concentrated. All she could think of was a time when she had been quite small and her father had taken her to the park playground at night. There had been a round, pale moon in the sky, and he had pushed her high on the swing, so high that he had told her, each time she rose to the top of the arc, "Touch the moon, Jennifer. Touch the moon with your toes." She had touched it too, or thought she had.

"How about Moontoucher?" she asked.

The stallion shook his head.

Jennifer looked nervously toward the house. The lights had come on. At least that would make it harder for anyone to see out. "Maybe we should just forget —"

"I know!" the nameless horse neighed, in a voice so shrill that Jennifer's hands flew to her ears. She looked, again, toward the house and cried, "Shhhh! Shhhhhhhh!"

"My name," he said, hardly more quietly, "is Moon-seeker!"

"Shhhh!" Jennifer said once more, but still she nodded, feeling rather pleased. She probably wouldn't have thought of Moonseeker herself, but it was really quite a classy name for a horse . . . for *her* horse. "All right. Moonseeker it is," she said. Then she added, wanting to hurry things along, "Are you ready now?"

"Of course," the horse answered instantly, but then he asked, "Ready for what?"

"To go for a run." Jennifer pointed down the gravel drive-way, past the side of the house, and out to the street. All she had to do was to get on his back and ride away, then she wouldn't have to worry about who saw Moonseeker or about getting called to come inside.

"Certainly. Let's go!" Moonseeker neighed. Without an-other word he pivoted and cantered off down the driveway, leaving an astonished Jennifer standing alone by the trees, still pointing the way.

chapter five

"Come back!" Jennifer yelled, forgetting about being heard in the house. "You have to give me a chance to get on."

Moonseeker slowed to a trot, then to a walk, and finally, almost at the end of the driveway, he stopped and turned around. He started back, walking with his head tipped to one side. "I have to do what?" he asked when he was in front of Jennifer again.

"You . . . have . . . to . . . give . . . me . . . a . . . chance . . . to . . . get . . . on."

"On?" he inquired. "On what?"

"On you!" she answered, thoroughly exasperated. "On your back!"

Moonseeker's skin rippled violently, almost as if it had a life of its own quite apart from the rest of the horse. "You mean to say you think you're going to sit on me? You want me to *carry* you about?"

"Of course! That's what horses are for. To let people ride them!"

Moonseeker retreated several steps. "That may be what *some* horses are for, but not this one." His voice was low and very certain.

Jennifer took a deep breath. What good was this going to be . . . to have a horse she couldn't ride? "But don't you see? If you don't let me ride you, we can't go anyplace together. You're so much bigger than I am, so much stronger, so much faster" — with each descriptive adjective Moonseeker's chest seemed to expand — "that I could never keep up. I'd be worn out before we reached the edge of town."

"I *am* very fast," he agreed, "and strong, too. And," he hesitated and looked at her inquiringly, "what else did you say?"

Conceited, she thought, but she said, "Big. You're big enough to carry someone much larger than me."

"Yes," he agreed. "You're right. I am."

Jennifer waited.

Moonseeker looked her up and down and curled his upper lip in that snide way he had. "You have such stubby legs. And only two of them."

"People are only supposed to have two legs," she answered crossly. Then, afraid she was losing the advantage she had gained, she added in a more conciliatory tone, "That's why we need horses."

"I'm sure you do," Moonseeker said imperiously. But then he paused and twitched his ears. "Now that I think of it, there was somebody who rode me once. I don't remember who it was, though."

Jennifer held her breath.

"All right, then. Get on," Moonseeker said as though riding had been his idea all along.

Jennifer looked up at the gigantic horse towering above her. She looked at his long, slender legs and his smooth sides with nothing to grab on to. He wasn't wearing a saddle, of course, or even a bridle, and he certainly didn't come with built-in steps. "Um," she said, "do you think you could kneel?"

"Kneel! You want *me* to kneel?" Moonseeker snorted with indignation.

"Well, it won't do any good if *I* kneel, will it?"

He peered down his long nose at her, his haughty stare making her scalp crinkle, and said, "You *are* awfully short."

She wanted to snap back, *I'm the second tallest girl in my class,* but knowing that wouldn't help anything and knowing that she was running out of time, she said instead, "Maybe I could find something to climb on."

Moonseeker nodded his head abruptly and ordered, "Then find something."

Jennifer tried several times, unsuccessfully, to climb onto Moonseeker's back. First from a stump. Too low. Then from her bicycle seat. Too tippy. Then from the back bumper of the car. Moonseeker wouldn't come far enough into the shadowy garage for her to use the car itself.

Finally she talked him into standing on the outer edge of the spruce trees again. One of her favorite tree games with Liz — apart from straddling a branch and pretending to ride — was sitting facing outward on a branch as if at the top of a sliding board and slipping its long, dipping length to the ground. She positioned Moonseeker carefully at the outer edge of one of the trees and slid down a higher branch then she usually chose, aiming for his back.

The first time she tried, she overshot Moonseeker entirely and landed on the ground with a bone-crunching thud.

"My, how clumsy humans are," he said, without even turning his head to see if she was in one piece.

At least we're not afraid of being imprisoned by spruce trees, Jennifer wanted to answer, but again she held her tongue. It was amazing, really. She ordinarily said everything that popped into her head. She certainly did when she was playing with Liz or talking to her brother. But in a few short minutes with this horse, she had learned a lesson her mother had been trying to teach her for as long as she could remember.

Think before you speak, her mother often said. *Think how your words are going to affect the other person.* Well, when the other "person" was a bossy, crabby, self-centered horse, and when you wanted to ride that horse more than anything in the world, you learned in a hurry.

On her second attempt, Jennifer chose a lower limb. She

backed down it for greater control, easing along until the branch began to dip, then letting herself build up speed until she dropped, none too lightly, onto Moonseeker's back.

"Oof!" he said. "You're all sharp corners!"

But if she was all sharp corners, he was entirely smooth curves. Her perch on his back felt more unreliable than she had ever imagined it could be. In the first place, Moonseeker's hide was as slippery as if it had been polished for sliding. In the second place, his back was broad, and she felt as if she were doing sideward splits. And in the third place, there was absolutely nothing to hang on to except the thick, cream-colored mane, and to do that from the middle of his back she had to lean foward so far that she was almost lying on her belly.

"Whoa!" she yelled when Moonseeker began to walk, jostling her so she slid from side to side at every step.

"Whoa?" He imitated her voice, adding a whining nicker that she knew sounded nothing like her at all. "But we've just started!" And he began to trot a little.

With each thudding trot, Jennifer flew up into the air and then was met again by Moonseeker's broad back and hard spine. He always seemed to be coming up just as she was coming down, and every time she landed, her teeth clattered together. She was certain the bones in her spine were clattering together too.

"I remember this now," Moonseeker said, moving into

the driveway and increasing his pace. "We've done this before, haven't we?"

What was he talking about? Jennifer couldn't begin to imagine. In fact, as she leaned forward, clinging to Moonseeker's mane, she knew that she had never done anything like this in her entire life . . . nor was she sure she wanted to be doing it now. Leaning forward, careening from side to side on the slippery back, she could see nothing but the gravel passing beneath flashing hooves. That gravel might have been a mile away, two miles. Would a parachute help? Already she could feel what it was going to be like to fall. But she didn't seem to be able to get her mouth working to try again to stop the stallion.

"This is almost like old times!" Moonseeker was exclaiming.

Jennifer twined her fingers through his mane and pulled herself forward until she could grip his neck with her elbows. "Stop!" she yelled. "Please, stop!"

Just short of the street, Moonseeker stopped. He stopped so abruptly that Jennifer almost didn't stop with him. In fact, the only thing which prevented her from sailing right over his head was the frantically tight hold she had on his mane. She ended up, however, hanging beneath his throat like an impossibly bulky necklace, her arms and legs wrapped tightly around his neck.

Moonseeker stood very still. "Do you think you're going to want to ride very far like that?" he inquired with a mild sweetness in his voice that made for better sarcasm.

Jennifer let go with her legs, reaching for the ground. When she didn't find it, she released her hold on Moonseeker's neck and dropped. Her knees buckled as she landed. They seemed to have been jellied. A pickup rattled past, incredibly not even slowing at the sight of this enormous horse standing practically in the street.

"I'm not riding anywhere like that," Jennifer said, her voice trembling. "I'm not riding anywhere with you at all if you're going to jounce so much."

"Jounce!" Moonseeker slapped his tail irritably from side to side. "I don't jounce. You don't know how to ride. You used to when you rode me before, but you've forgotten."

Jennifer leaned over and rubbed her legs. What was this obnoxious animal talking about? If he was the same horse she used to ride when she played with Liz, why was his name Moonseeker, not Pretty Girl? And how could anyone — even a talking horse—remember something that hadn't really happened?

She straightened up again slowly. She might as well try a little truth. They weren't getting anywhere like this. "I never rode before," she admitted, "except for pretend . . . and pretend doesn't seem to help." In fact, her father's offer of riding lessons was sounding better all the time.

She waited to see what Moonseeker would do. Maybe he would run off and leave her the way he had started to before. Maybe he would be so disgusted that he would refuse to let her on his back again, even if he stayed.

But to her surprise he merely sighed with the aggrieved

patience of a too-busy parent and said, "In that case, I guess I'm going to have to teach you."

So they went back to the spruce tree, and Jennifer selected the same branch that had worked before, and again she landed on Moonseeker's back. This time, though, she managed to find a spot just behind his massive shoulders which allowed her to sit up straight and still grasp the base of his mane.

"Now, hang on with your legs," Moonseeker commanded.

"With my legs?" Jennifer squeaked, but she pressed her knees into his sides and was surprised to see how the gripping of her legs could steady her. When Moonseeker began walking again, she stayed firmly upright. After a moment, she leaned forward, keeping a tight grip with her knees, and said urgently, "Let's head out of town."

Moonseeker stopped at the end of the driveway to consider the street, standing in full view of the front of the house.

"Let's go," Jennifer urged. "That way!" She tugged his mane to try to make him face the way she wanted to go and banged on his sides with her feet the way she had seen people do in movies. There was nothing to stop him, not even a single car in the street, but he stood peering into the gathering dusk and didn't move. "Hurry!" Jennifer pleaded. She was watching the front door.

But even as she spoke, it swung open.

Jennifer's mother stepped out onto the front steps, her mouth already formed for calling. "Jennifer!"

As if in response to her mother's voice, the streetlights up and down the street flicked on, the one nearest where Moonseeker stood casting a pool of light which illuminated them like a spotlight in the middle of a stage. Since there seemed nothing else to be done, Jennifer sat completely still and waited for her mother to react to what she was seeing.

But her mother didn't react. She looked directly at the end of the driveway and at the streetlight and at Jennifer atop the huge horse as if there were nothing to be seen. Then she turned and faced the other direction, calling again, "Jennifer!"

Jennifer couldn't breathe. Her name rang through the still air one more time, and then her mother, obviously exasperated, stepped back into the house, shutting the door with a bang.

chapter six

"She didn't see us!" Jennifer whispered. "She didn't see us at all!"

"Of course not," Moonseeker replied. "I told you. No one can see me."

"But *I* see you," she objected.

"That's different."

"Why . . . why is it different?"

"I don't know," Moonseeker answered irritably. "It just is. Because you used to dream me, I guess. Because you *wanted* to see me."

Jennifer touched Moonseeker's solid neck, then the equally firm flesh of her own arm. "When I'm on your back," she asked, "am I invisible too?"

"Of course," Moonseeker answered. "What did you think?"

What had she thought? That she wanted a horse . . .

nothing more. And now she had one. A horse no one else could see couldn't possibly be taken away. "I think," she said, "that we should go for a ride."

Moonseeker nodded and started down the street, increasing his speed almost immediately to a brisk trot. With the first abrupt movement of the trot, Jennifer flew into the air. When she landed, she thought she was going to split in two. "Oh," she cried. And as she came down from each successive bounce, "Oh, oh, oh."

But just when she knew she was going to be rattled into pieces, he called, "Now, for some real speed," and to Jennifer's amazement—and relief—the movement smoothed out, became more of a long, gliding, rocking motion. After a few minutes she was able to flow, pretty well, with the gallop, even to look around a little.

It took them only minutes to reach the edge of town. Moonseeker galloped past Liz's house, past the library and the school, past the Texaco Service Station and the lumberyard. At first Jennifer worried about cars. Since the drivers couldn't see them, she was afraid of being hit. It wasn't as if Moonseeker could pass through walls. The branches of the spruce trees had been enough to cause a problem. But she needn't have worried. The streets were nearly empty, and Moonseeker kept a careful distance from the occasional passing car. Several teenagers were hanging around in front of the Will Hop Inn on the very edge of town, but no one batted an eye when they thundered past.

"Moonseeker," she called, thinking she didn't want to get too far from home. But either he was so busy running, the wind flattening his ears, that he didn't hear his own name, or else he was just refusing to listen. In either case, Jennifer didn't have much choice but to hang on and to go wherever he went.

A short distance past the edge of town, they came to a cornfield, and to Jennifer's great astonishment, Moonseeker sailed across the drainage ditch along the side of the road. Before she could right herself from that landing, he asked, galloping toward a pasture beyond the cornfield and the barbed wire fence surrounding it, "What's that?"

"It's a fence," Jennifer gasped, leaning forward and closing her eyes. "Don't—"

But Moonseeker replied, "Oh, I've jumped those before. I remember." And he launched his entire body into the air with a single powerful spring.

For an instant Jennifer wasn't sure whether he had left her behind or sent her on ahead. The only thing she knew for certain was that she was sailing over the fence on her own, entirely separated from her mount. She landed, quite incredibly, on her hands and feet and rolled in the soft pasture grass.

"Why did you get off?" Moonseeker demanded, circling back, peering down at her from his great height.

"Get off!" Jennifer screamed, scrambling to her feet. "Who got off? You threw me!"

Moonseeker tossed his head. "Did I?" he asked, his voice filled with admiration for his own power.

"Crud!" Jennifer exclaimed, examining herself for wounds. There was a tear in one knee of her new slacks. "You're the dumbest horse I've ever seen!"

Moonseeker took a step backwards, the whites showing around his dark eyes. "I am not. I'm not the least bit dumb. In fact, every minute I remember something else that I know."

"Well, it's dumb to jump a fence when your rider doesn't know what you're going to do!"

"But I told you I was going to jump," he objected.

"Not in time to give me anything to say about it. I don't know how to jump. You might have killed me!"

But if Moonseeker had any concern about killing her, it didn't show. He swished his tail, stamped his heavy hooves, and said impatiently, "I was the one who did the jumping, not you."

"Yeah," Jennifer replied. "And I was the one who did the flying."

The great, golden horse snorted, but then he asked, his tone more subdued if not exactly humble, "What is it you need to know?"

"What I need to know," Jennifer said in exasperation, "is how to stay on."

"Oh."

Then she added, looking around, "And how to get back

on now. We're a long way from the spruce trees."

Moonseeker gazed around too. They both ended up facing several curious cows staring at them from the other side of the pasture. (Apparently Moonseeker wasn't invisible to cows.)

Moonseeker tossed his head, backed up, danced in place. But then he asked, trying to be nonchalant, "Why are those horses so short and so funny looking?"

"Because they aren't horses, they're cows," Jennifer replied crossly, "and if you think I'm going to climb on one of them to reach you, you've got another think coming." Moonseeker did stand enough taller than any of the cows that it might have been possible—assuming the cow stood still and the palomino stallion didn't frighten himself out of his wits walking up to them—but he already had another idea.

"Over there," he said, nodding toward a pile of hay bales, and Jennifer trailed him reluctantly to the stack, climbed it, and swung her leg over his back again. If she had any sense at all, she would walk home. But instead she retied her grandmother's scarf around her neck and adjusted Brad's light on her belt. "I'm ready for my first jumping lesson," she told Moonseeker.

"No six-foot fences," Moonseeker promised.

Jennifer looked back at the fence they had come over. It wasn't anywhere near six feet, but she wasn't going to tell him that. Besides, she remembered a bit guiltily that when she played at riding in the spruce tree she was always pretending to jump things that were six-feet high. In fact, Liz had complained sometimes that Jennifer and Pretty Girl were the only ones who got the interesting jumps.

"We'll start with some easy ones," Moonseeker announced, "even though *I'm* capable of much more."

Jennifer decided not to argue the point.

They practiced first with some hay bales lying apart from the rest of the stack, Moonseeker calling instructions all the time. The role of teacher obviously suited him perfectly. It gave him a chance to tell her exactly what to do every minute.

"I feel more balanced when you lean forward," he told her. "Now squeeze with your legs."

Jennifer was getting tired of being told, "Squeeze with your legs," but she liked even less the idea of falling off again, so she squeezed. She had never realized that riding was such hard work. Always before she had thought you simply sat up there and left everything to the horse.

But if Moonseeker was a bossy teacher, he wasn't exactly a patient one, and after several small jumps over hay bales, he began running toward a pile of brush several times higher than a single bale.

"That's too high," Jennifer shouted. When it was obvious that he was going to jump it anyway (she might have figured! he didn't care what happened to her), she closed her eyes and leaned almost over his neck, squeezing with her legs as hard as she could.

To her amazement she stayed on this time. And when she remembered to open her eyes, they were rocketing along toward the other end of the pasture, descending a gentle slope.

Thank goodness there didn't seem to be a fence at this end, and after leaping a puddle and one small boulder, Moonseeker settled into the business of running instead of jumping. His warm, sleek body moved beneath her as though it were part of her own, and the wind riffled her hair and tugged at her scarf.

There was nothing like riding. Nothing in the world! And Moonseeker was a wonderful horse! It didn't matter where he had come from, how he had gotten here. It didn't even matter that he was sometimes rude. He was hers. She would ride him like this every day. Her parents could hardly say no to a horse they couldn't even see.

The sky had darkened to a slate gray, and Venus, the evening star, was visible just above the horizon. Jennifer started to wish on it, "Star light, star bright . . . ," but then she stopped. What was there left to wish for? She had everything she had ever wanted.

A new smell permeated the air, and Jennifer breathed deeply. Instead of dried hay and the warm sweetness of the cattle and the fragrance of the bruised grass beneath Moonseeker's feet, there was the musky, fish-laced scent of water, a faint murmur of water, too.

She remembered then. There was a river somewhere over here. It was where Brad had gathered her tadpoles last year.

It was where he and his friends often came to fish. Her parents had said that she would be allowed to come here, too, when she was old enough. Surely eleven would be old enough. If she didn't stay out too late this evening and get herself into too much trouble, they would let her do lots of things now.

"Don't you think," she shouted, leaning over Moonseeker's neck so she could get as close as possible to his ear — she still hadn't decided whether he couldn't hear her when he was running or if he simply ignored her — "that we should go — "

She was going to say *home,* but before the word was out of her mouth, the river loomed in front of them, dark and wet and very wide.

"Watch out!" she yelled.

"What is it?" Moonseeker asked, and to Jennifer's enormous relief, he swerved to run along the bank.

"It's a river," she told him. And then she added, in case he needed to be told, "It's very wet."

But to Jennifer's dismay, Moonseeker replied, tossing his head, "Oh, I've jumped rivers before . . . lots of times."

Jennifer couldn't think of a single time in her play that she had pretended to jump a river, but she didn't know how she was going to convince Moonseeker of that. Besides, even if he had jumped pretend rivers, that didn't mean he could make it across a real one.

"But . . ." she started to say. "But . . . but . . ." Then she stuttered into silence.

Moonseeker continued to gallop along the bank without the slightest hesitation in his step, one eye on the river. On their left a bluff was beginning to loom. On their right, Venus was reflected on the surface of the dark water as a small, silvery white smear.

"Look!" Moonseeker called, his voice high with delight. "The moon! I can jump the river and touch the moon at the same time!"

"But that's not . . ." Jennifer started to say, wondering where he had gotten the idea of touching the moon anyway. "That's only a —"

Before she could get all the words out, though, Moonseeker cried, "Here I go!" and thrust himself into the air in the direction of the opposite riverbank.

For an instant Jennifer thought, *We're flying. We're going to make it!* but that was followed immediately with, *We're falling. We're going to drown!* And the next thing she knew there was a splash like an enormous tree falling into the water and she was floating free of Moonseeker's back, still gripping his mane with one tightly clenched hand and beating frantically at the enveloping water with the other.

chapter seven

When Moonseeker's head broke through the black water, he was screaming, a high, shrieking whinny that splintered the air. There were no words this time, simply the inarticulate cry of any terrified horse.

"Swim!" Jennifer shouted, still clinging with one hand to his mane and thrashing at the water with the other. "You've got to swim!"

"I don't know how!" Moonseeker bleated.

"Kick your legs!" Jennifer ordered, grateful that she was a strong swimmer, wondering how you performed a lifesaving maneuver on a horse. But even as she said it, Moonseeker was beginning, instinctively, to move his legs, to swim haltingly back toward the riverbank.

"That's it," Jennifer soothed, keeping her hold on his mane. "Just keep kicking." As she spoke, she heard one of

Moonseeker's hooves scrape against a rock, and then he was scrambling to his feet, stumbling toward dry land, leaving her to follow as best she could.

"Stupid horse," she muttered, for what felt like the hundredth time as she trudged out of the water in his foaming wake. Dank river water streamed from her hair, and her new pink slacks and matching striped top pressed against her skin, sodden and cold.

She took Brad's bicycle light off her belt and shook it. It seemed dry. She turned it on, then off again. It was probably the only birthday present she had gotten that wasn't ruined. What a birthday this was turning out to be! Maybe her father had known what he was doing when he had refused to give her a live horse.

Moonseeker lurched up the bank and then stood, his legs spraddled like a graceless colt, and shook himself violently. Jennifer waited until he was done before she pulled herself up by a bush that grew close to the water.

"What do we do next?" Moonseeker asked, slapping his wet tail from side to side and giving a last flick to his mane.

"Well, I don't know what *you're* going to do," Jennifer replied, crossly, "but *I'm* going home. I'm tired and I'm wet and this isn't fun anymore." Her throat tightened as she spoke. Surely she wasn't going to cry in front of this big lug of a horse!

Moonseeker lowered his head and peered into her face. "But this is your birthday," he said, and Jennifer didn't know whether its being her birthday meant that she shouldn't be tired and wet or that she shouldn't want to go home.

"You've always wanted a real horse," he added softly.

"I don't think you even know how to be a horse," Jennifer replied, not the least bit mollified. "No horse in the world would have tried to jump that river."

"But . . . but . . . I've jumped rivers like that before. I know I have. I don't know what happened this time." It was a statement, but it sounded more like a question.

Jennifer sighed. She felt, suddenly, extremely tired, tired of explaining things, tired of being responsible for this creature. "If you did, that was just pretend," she said. "Don't you know the difference between pretend and real life?"

"No." His head drooped lower. "I guess I don't."

Jennifer hesitated. How could she explain it? "Real life," she said at last, "is what you can really do. Pretend is just what you wish you could do."

"And I can't really jump a river?" Moonseeker's nose almost touched the ground between his front hooves.

"No!" Jennifer looked at the dejected animal and repeated more gently, "No horse could. Maybe somebody used to pretend you could . . . like I used to pretend I could ride, better than anybody else, especially better than Liz. I used to pretend we were the most fantastic pair in town, you and I, but it didn't mean anything, really."

"Am *I* pretend?" Moonseeker asked, his voice very soft, and Jennifer looked at him in surprise.

"I don't know," she answered honestly. But then she stepped forward and laid one hand on his warm, wet flank. "I don't see how you could be, really. You're here, aren't you?"

"I think so," he said dolefully, "but I guess I'm not absolutely sure."

As they stood there, side by side on the riverbank, stars were beginning to break through the darkening sky with their pinpricks of light. The moon hadn't risen yet, so the night was growing very dark.

Jennifer said, "I guess we'd better be getting back. My parents will worry." She looked around. "But I don't know how I'm going to get on you again."

"Perhaps," the mighty horse answered, still in that same gentle voice, "it would help if I knelt."

And he did. He bent his front legs, lowering himself until Jennifer could clamber up, just behind his shoulders. Then he stood again with a lurch that almost unseated her, but she clung tightly and stayed on.

"Which way?" Moonseeker asked, and Jennifer looked around. "Away from the river," she directed. That had to be back toward home.

Moonseeker nodded and began plodding forward in the darkness, entirely subdued now. Jennifer patted his neck to try to reassure him. She wondered as she did if she didn't prefer Moonseeker when he was bossy and rash and entirely too stuck on himself.

A light breeze had sprung up, and she shivered in her wet clothes. Though she could see little, either in front of them or around, she wasn't worried. They would have to come to the pasture again soon . . . and then to the fence and the road. Maybe Moonseeker should be turning more to the left. They had probably moved downriver a ways trying to get out of the water, and she remembered having seen a bluff emerge just back from the riverbank. They might be about to walk into a cliff face. The darkness in front of them certainly seemed to be impenetrable.

"Moonseeker," she said, but even as she bent over to speak, a large, prickly bush brushed her leg and Moonseeker's side. Moonseeker shied away from it only to stumble into another bush on the other side. In response to the clawing tendrils of that bush, he bolted straight into the darkness they had been approaching, running a dozen or more steps before slowing to a walk again.

Jennifer closed her eyes, expecting the dark air they plunged through to turn into a solid wall. When nothing happened, she opened them, pleased that she had managed to keep her seat. She leaned over to pat Moonseeker's neck, to try to soothe him again. What was it that made him so afraid of being surrounded closely with anything?

Moonseeker's hooves were beginning to make a hollow, clopping noise quite unlike the soft thudding they had made on the riverbank. The sound bounced back eerily. The night seemed to be growing darker with each step. Jennifer looked up. She couldn't see stars anymore.

Moonseeker stopped moving. Jennifer held herself stiffly quiet. Even the air around them was still. There was no trace of the breeze that had been chilling her a minute before although it was still damp and cool.

"Where are we?" Jennifer asked, and the end of her sentence bounced back to her with a thin, hollow ring. "Are we?"

Wherever they were, they were no longer in the open night air, and they were no longer moving along the riverbank toward home.

chapter eight

Moonseeker stamped his feet, and the sound of the stamping bounced back to them like the beating of a drum.

When that had quieted, he said, "We're trapped. We've walked into something . . . some place."

"Some place . . . place," repeated the echo.

"Maybe a cave," Jennifer suggested, trying to keep her voice calm, though she was feeling far from calm. "I've heard Brad talk about caves in the river bluffs."

They both stayed quiet and attentive, listening to the hollow repetition of the word *bluffs*.

"Why don't we turn around?" Jennifer whispered, hoping to defeat the echo, but her words hissed back as though returned by a snake.

Obediently, Moonseeker began to turn, but the moment

he took a sidewards step, just a small one, he came up against a stony wall. He stopped, his skin shuddering in such waves that Jennifer thought she was going to be rippled off onto the ground.

"Try the other way." She spoke aloud this time, preferring the repetition of her final word, *way*, to the sibilance of the snake.

Moonseeker began pivoting slowly in the other direction, but in about two careful sidewards steps, he came up against another wall. He stopped short, saying nothing, though he was beginning to tremble violently.

"Moonseeker"—Jennifer spoke quietly—"can you back up?"

He took a step backwards, stumbled, brushed up against something—perhaps a wall, maybe only the bush they had passed at the mouth of the cave—and bolted forward again. Jennifer clung to his mane as he lurched ahead, stopping and starting in sudden erratic bursts, running a dozen steps, two dozen, twisting and turning in response to the winding of the dark passage that had trapped them. As Moonseeker stumbled on, the walls seemed to move closer. He might have been running into a funnel.

"Stop!" Jennifer yelled, and the echo yelled, too. "*Stop!*"

Moonseeker stopped, but whether because he had obeyed or because he was now too tightly wedged to move, Jennifer couldn't tell. Again he stood perfectly still, his breath coming in snorting gasps. How could such a big horse be so easily frightened?

But then she remembered. If the darkness was what was frightening him, she had a solution for that. She had the bicycle lamp Brad had given her. Thank goodness it hadn't taken in water. She removed it from her belt.

"Look!" she said, and she held the lamp up and switched it on. A beam of light illuminated the long, stone passage they were in, the close-fitting, gray walls, the low ceiling — she had been lucky not to have had her head cracked open when Moonseeker was running.

"Turn it off!" Moonseeker screamed, and he reared so that Jennifer had to bend over quickly, turning off the light as she ducked.

"What's wrong?" she asked when he had settled again. "Don't you want to see?"

"No! That makes it worse."

Jennifer could feel her back slump as if the stiffening were going out of her spine. There was nothing she could do. She and Moonseeker were going to be trapped in this cave forever.

She bent over his neck, stroked it, tried to keep her voice calm. "If you can't back up, can you walk straight ahead, slowly and carefully? We're bound to come to some place where you can turn around."

"I can't," he replied in a voice that quavered back to them from the walls of the dark, surrounding cave. "I just can't. It's too close!"

"Are you stuck?" she asked, trying to feel down his side. There seemed to be enough room for him to move.

Moonseeker's only reply was "It's too dark. It's just like it was before."

"Before? Before when?"

"Before I came to you," Moonseeker answered crossly, as if the answer were obvious, as if she should understand everything he said without explanation.

"But where were you . . . before?" Jennifer wanted very much to understand.

Moonseeker shuddered. "I don't know where it was. Everything used to be dark, tight. The walls were close. There was this dry, tickly stuff all around me. I waited and waited and waited. I thought I'd never get out."

The box! That was what Moonseeker was talking about. He could remember being the china horse enclosed inside the box, surrounded by paper straw. That was why he was afraid of the dark, why he had been afraid of the enclosing branches of the spruce trees.

And strangely enough, he could remember, too, being Pretty Girl, her pretend horse. He could even remember the games they used to play, the things she made up. Six-foot fences, for instance. Being a horse who could do anything. Being a horse and rider who never once had to think of anybody else.

And strangest of all — and the part she still didn't understand — he could remember doing things she had never done with him at all . . . like jumping the river, like trying to touch the moon.

"I have an idea," she said, leaning forward and speaking softly, as close to his ear as she could get. "Remember when I led you out from the spruce trees?"

He nodded his head.

"Remember how I tied my birthday scarf around your eyes so you wouldn't see the branches, and then you weren't afraid?"

Again a nod, less emphatic this time.

"Well, I can do that again . . . right now." She leaned farther forward, pulling off her wet scarf, and wrapped it carefully around Moonseeker's head. She felt to make sure she had covered his eyes. "Now," she said, "it's not dark anymore. There's nothing too close around you anymore. You've got your eyes closed, that's all. Like when I took care of you before."

Moonseeker snorted lightly, flicked his tail so that it hit first one side of the cave, then the other.

Oh dear, Jennifer thought. *Don't do that! You'll never forget the walls that way!* But she could feel his withers relax beneath her hands.

"Now," she said, continuing her instructions in her most soothing voice, "you must stand very still, because I'm going to get down, and I'll be standing right by your feet."

She turned on the light and slid to the floor of the cave. Then she stood, almost beneath Moonseeker's belly, and shone the light this way and that. Behind them seemed to be blank wall. Apparently Moonseeker had come around corners during his last frantic dash. She would never be able to back him out through such twists and turns. The first time he bumped into a wall, he would panic again.

She shone the light ahead. The passage continued, long and straight, just about wide enough and tall enough for a horse and a not-too-tall rider. Maybe they should try that way first, see what was up ahead. There might even be a place to turn around . . . or an exit at the other end. She sighed deeply, but she moved along carefully to Moonseeker's head and took him by the forelock. (His head was so bowed in his dejection that she didn't have to ask him to lower it so she could reach.) But when she tugged, he didn't move.

"Come on," she said. "You've got to follow me . . . the way you did before."

In response, however, Moonseeker simply braced himself against her, his legs splayed, his ears flattened against his head. "You can't trick me," he said. "I've seen what it's like."

Jennifer's hands twitched with irritation. She had had about all she could take. "Then how about backing up? We'll go out the way we came in."

Moonseeker simply shook his head.

Jennifer wanted to stamp her feet, to shout at him. In fact, she wanted to kick him in the shins . . . if the front of a horse's legs were called shins. This was too much . . . entirely. She would take herself home and leave Moonseeker here. It wouldn't be any worse for him than spending the last few years in her grandmother's drawer.

But Moonseeker was trembling so violently that his mane and tail shook, and Jennifer couldn't make herself walk away.

Perhaps she could go just briefly, run back to town to get her father. She knew, though, that it would take her a long time to get back on her own legs, and Moonseeker might do himself some harm while she was gone. Besides, even if she made her father believe that she had a real horse in a cave by the river, what would he do when he arrived and saw nothing at all? How could anybody rescue a horse except the one who could see it?

Jennifer turned and shone the light down the passage that lay ahead. "Wait," she said softly, "just wait. I'm going a few steps ahead." Maybe something she saw would give her an idea.

Moonseeker said nothing. The great horse simply stood there in the darkness, shivering as if from cold.

Jennifer followed the flat circle of light, pretending it could lead her somewhere, though where she was going — except that it was deeper into the cave — she had no idea. She stopped, finally, when she discovered in one wall, just above her head, a small ledge. She looked at the ledge, then at the round face of the lamp in her hand and she had an idea.

What if she could convince Moonseeker that the moon waited for them farther up the passage, that he could touch it if he moved on a short distance?

She stepped up into a foothold partway up the wall,

reaching as high as she could. She could just barely manage to put the bicycle lamp on the ledge, facing it back toward where Moonseeker stood.

Then she retraced her steps to Moonseeker and turned to give the lamp a considering look. It shone back at her, a clear, round light. But because it was shining directly at her, it didn't illuminate the confining cave, only presented itself as a distant goal. She uncovered Moonseeker's eyes.

"Look," she said, pointing toward the dazzling lamp in the distance. "We must have found the cave where the moon sleeps. Do you see it up there? It's so close, I'll bet you could touch it if you tried."

Moonseeker blinked. "Could I?" he asked, his head coming up slightly and his tail rising to attention too. "Do you really think I could?"

"Of course," Jennifer answered, "because you're that kind of a horse. Why do you think you're named Moonseeker?"

Moonseeker threw out his chest, just a little, and pawed the cave floor with one hoof.

"The moon is right there . . . waiting for you," Jennifer said, and the cave repeated softly, "For you."

Moonseeker neighed, first a tentative, wavering sound. Then he repeated it more forcefully until a symphony of neighing came back to them from the cave walls. "I'm going to touch the moon," he said, and barely containing himself to keep from running over Jennifer, he began stepping eagerly toward the light.

chapter nine

Moonseeker followed Jennifer toward the bicycle lamp, his hooves ringing on the stone floor. Jennifer walked slowly, trying to ignore his looming presence behind her and the streams of warm horse breath that parted her hair. She had to have time to think.

What would she say when they reached the light and Moonseeker found out what it was? What would she have accomplished by bringing him deeper into the cave? There was still no hint of any place to turn a big stallion around, and even if there was an opening at the other end, she would never get Moonseeker to move again once he knew she had tricked him. Her head buzzed with the problems. Her only hope was to get a chance to move the bicycle light again, keep doing it until they finally came to a wider place in the cave, then do it all the way back until they reached the cave mouth.

"Wait!" she commanded as they drew close to the high shelf where she had put the light.

"But . . . but . . ." Moonseeker stamped his feet. "We're nearly there. I can tell we are!"

"Wait!" Jennifer repeated, using her most authoritative voice. "We've got to be careful. Sometimes the moon has guards when it sleeps, you know." And she turned back to the stallion and held up, again, the angora scarf. "You close your eyes. I'll go up ahead to check."

At first she thought he was going to refuse. His nostrils widened and he rolled his eyes. But then he said, quite meekly for him, "Guards?" and lowered his head. "Will I be safe with my eyes closed?"

"Perfectly safe." Jennifer tied the scarf, smiling wryly to herself. Dark was obviously not the only thing that scared this big baby of a horse. "Now wait here," she told him. "I'll be right back . . . as soon as I'm sure everything's all right."

"I'm not afraid of guards," Moonseeker said, but he spoke in a near whisper and seemed to draw back from the echo of the word *guards* that bounced back at him from the cave walls.

Jennifer moved ahead carefully, keeping one hand on the wall as she walked because she couldn't see much facing the light as she was. She smiled even more broadly to herself. It would be rather nice, once they got home, to tell Moonseeker about the trick she had played. She was going to enjoy that.

She came to the shelf where she had left the bicycle lamp

and stepped up into the foothold to reach it down. But just as she grasped the light, her foot slipped and she thumped back to the cave floor, her elbow scraping the rough wall. The light flew out of her hand and landed on the hard floor with a metallic crunch. Everything went dark.

Jennifer caught her breath. Blackness lay around her like a cloak, solid and impenetrable. She knelt, scrabbling on the floor, feeling in every direction for the bicycle lamp. When she finally found it, she clicked the switch, clicked it again, shook the lamp until it rattled. Nothing happened. Her heart was pounding so loudly in her ears that she almost expected to hear the sound of it bounce back from the cave walls. This was too much! She couldn't take any more. She had to get out of here.

Moonseeker could take care of himself!

Clutching the useless light, she turned back the way she had come, stumbling, half running, trailing her hand along the wall to keep her direction. She tripped, almost fell down, gathered herself again, kept moving. Her breath was coming in ragged gasps.

"Is something wrong?" Moonseeker called in a thin, frightened voice.

"No," she panted, "nothing," just as she collided with his front legs. She was going to keep on running. She couldn't stop. It was ridiculous to keep moving deeper into the cave anyway, and she could manage to find her own way out . . . even without the light. She didn't owe Moonseeker a thing. He wasn't a real horse anyway. A horse who could appear when you dropped a china figurine, a horse whom no one could see except her, a horse who could talk, couldn't possibly be real. Her father had given her riding lessons . . . riding lessons and an old china toy. And her mother had given her clothes; her grandmother, an angora scarf; Brad, a bicycle light that no longer worked. No one had given her a real horse. No one!

But as she tried to brush past Moonseeker, she could feel the trembling warmth of his silken side, the frightened heaving of his breath, and she stumbled to a stop, leaning against him, closing her eyes against the overwhelming darkness.

"Touch the moon," her father had said when she was little enough to believe him. "Touch the moon with your toes." And she had done it.

Did believing make something real?

"Jennifer?" Moonseeker asked in the smallest voice anyone could imagine coming out of such a big horse. "Did the guards hurt you?"

Jennifer sighed. She could tell Moonseeker that the moon had run away, but that wouldn't be much help. They would still be caught in the darkness of the cave.

"No, of course not," she replied, opening her eyes. She would have to tell him something . . . for his own good. She had always thought before now that everything was either the truth or a lie, real or pretend, but everything she thought she had known was mixed up. She moved tiredly toward Moonseeker's head.

It was then that she saw for the first time something she

hadn't been able to see against the shining bicycle lamp . . . or in her frightened retreat. A glowing, silver-white ball of light seemed to be peering into the cave.

It was . . . Amazing! It was the moon. There must be an exit ahead, and the moon, just rising, shone beyond it with a clear, beckoning light.

Jennifer took a deep breath and reached up to lay her hand on the side of the stallion's warm neck. "I've got some bad news," she said quietly, "and some wonderful news."

"Yes?" Moonseeker replied, his entire body quiveringly alert.

"The moon has run away," Jennifer said.

Moonseeker's head dropped as if his neck had gone suddenly limp. "What's the wonderful news?" he asked in a tone that said very clearly he didn't think it could be wonderful at all.

Jennifer could feel the smile stretching her cheeks. "It's waiting for us just outside the cave. The moon is going to show us the way out."

Moonseeker came together as if he had been one of those jumping-jack horses controlled by a tightened string. "Why didn't you say so in the first place?" he demanded.

Jennifer didn't respond to that. Instead she said, reaching up to remove her grandmother's scarf, "It won't be as bright now, because it's farther away. But the moon's out there, waiting."

Moonseeker stood very still, examining the pale light that

shone at the end of the long tunnel of the cave. "Will I still be able to touch it?" he asked.

"Of course." Jennifer found a foothold in the wall and hoisted herself up onto his back. "We'll touch the moon together . . . you and I."

Moonseeker began to move, tentatively at first, then faster and with more authority. Finally he broke into a gallop, the sound of his hoofbeats reverberating from the cave walls like the accompaniment of a drum corps.

When he burst out of the other end of the cave, the glowing orb hung there in the sky like a welcoming friend, and Jennifer was certain, when he leapt, that they did touch the moon's cool face . . . both of them.

chapter ten

The trip home was easy. Jennifer and Moonseeker emerged from the cave very close to the highway they had followed out of town earlier, and all they had to do was to follow the same road back to Jennifer's house.

Jennifer slid off Moonseeker's back right next to the spruce trees. "I hope my parents haven't been worried," she said.

"I touched the moon," Moonseeker whinnied, prancing in the grass and tossing his head. "*I* touched the moon!"

"We both did," Jennifer replied, a bit startled by his display, though she knew that by now she shouldn't be.

"But you only touched it because you were on my back," the horse replied. "I'm the one who did it."

Jennifer shook her head. Some people . . . some horses never changed, no matter how much they went through.

"You're the one who did it," she agreed, and she put her arms around his neck and pressed her cheek against his sleek, warm hide. And then she added, more for herself than for him, "And you're my horse."

Just then she heard the back door open and her father calling, "Jennifer . . . Jennifer, are you out there?"

"Oh," Moonseeker said, apparently in response to her father's call, and his velvet-soft coat suddenly seemed less substantial against Jennifer's cheek.

"I think," he said, even his voice growing thinner, "that means I have to go."

Jennifer was stunned. *Have to go!* But she wanted Moonseeker to be hers forever! She clung more tightly to his neck, twining her fingers through his thick, silky mane.

"You can't," she said, her words strained and tight. "I won't let you."

"Jennifer!" her father called again.

"Here, Daddy," she answered back, "by the trees." Maybe her father could help. Even if he couldn't see Moonseeker, there must be something he could do. When she explained about her invisible horse, he would tell Moonseeker it was all right for him to stay. He would even find a stable and some hay and a bucket of fresh water. Together they would get a brush and brush the palomino's golden coat. If they did that, her father would have to see Moonseeker too, and whatever her father saw would be real for certain.

But Moonseeker had other ideas, or perhaps he had no

ideas at all, perhaps he wasn't in charge of what was going on. Because as her father approached, Moonseeker faded within the circle of Jennifer's arms from being a warm, living beast to a shimmering mist shaped like a horse.

Jennifer tried to grab his mane more firmly, but even that seemed to dissolve. First it was coarse, slippery hair, then it was water, then fog, a silken coolness against her fingers. She found herself grasping air, hanging on tightly to nothing at all. Moonseeker had disappeared.

"Where have you been, Jennifer? Your mother and I have been looking everywhere." Her father's voice was cross and relieved at the same time.

Jennifer took a step away from her father, reaching all around her, trying to touch something . . . anything at all. Maybe Moonseeker was still there, still solid, and had just, for the moment, become invisible to her. Then her hands fell to her sides, empty.

She turned to face her father, her eyes blurry with tears, but he had stopped speaking, stopped moving, and was staring at her.

"Criminey!" he exclaimed. "What happened to you? You're dirty . . . and wet!" He plucked at the sleeve of her shirt. "Your new slacks are torn, and your elbow is bleeding!" He held her arm tightly, just above the place where she had scraped it on the cave wall. "Jennifer?"

Jennifer shook her head, brushed at her cheeks with her free hand. What could she tell him? She stared at the grass, unable to look at his face. But then she saw, between them on the ground where Moonseeker had been standing, the china horse, still whole, still perfectly formed. She stooped to pick it up.

"Ah," her father said, when he saw the figurine in her hand, "Moonseeker."

"You know his name." She said it flatly, but inside her head the words sang. *Her father knew Moonseeker's name!* She held the china figure higher so the sleek, golden coat glimmered in the moonlight.

Her father nodded. "Of course. I named him." He reached out to stroke the proud arch of the tiny neck with an extended index finger.

"And did you and he . . . did you . . . ?"

His finger touched her lips gently, silencing her. "Perhaps," he told her, "we had best concentrate on what we'll say to your mother."

Jennifer took a deep, trembling breath and nodded. "A rainstorm?" she offered, looking down at her wet clothes.

He laughed. "In the backyard? One that didn't appear around front?"

Jennifer laughed too and wiped her eyes with one end of the lavender scarf her grandmother had knitted for her. The scarf was soggy, but it was still fragrant with the good, dusty, nose-twitching smell of horse. "Here, Daddy," she said. "Smell."

He bent over the scarf, smiling. And even in the darkness

that smile shared everything which had not been spoken. *I am happy for you*, it seemed to say. *You have found my horse.*

Out loud he said only, "I suppose we'll have to tell your mother you went for a little walk in the country . . . and came back again."

"Tell her I touched the moon," Jennifer said, and her father laughed again, then took her hand, and together they began to walk to the house.

Jennifer pulled to a stop at the steps. "Was he real?" she asked. "Will he come back?"

Her father stopped next to her, but he answered only, "Now those are two very different questions."

"But—" she started to respond, and he interrupted.

"And I'm not sure I have the answer to either one."

They both stood looking down at the golden horse Jennifer held. "I'm going to put him on my windowsill," she said.

"Where he can always see the moon," her father finished for her.

Jennifer put her arms around her father's waist and hugged him, hard. "You know, Daddy," she said, "your dream horse is the best birthday present I've ever had."

He returned the hug, saying nothing. But Jennifer was certain that she heard, from behind his back where the china toy was cupped carefully but not too tightly in her hand, a tiny voice which neighed, "Of course, I'm the best. What did you expect?"